Hawai'i

MOLOKA'I

MAUI

LĀNA'I

KAHO'OLAWE

HAWAI'I

"Surf's Up For Kimo"

Written by Kerry Germain
Illustrated by Keoni Montes

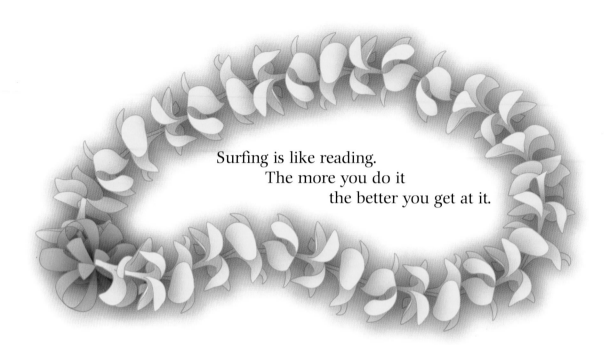

Surfing is like reading.
The more you do it
    the better you get at it.

Copyright 2000 Text by Kerry Germain
Copyright 2000 Art by Keoni Montes
ISBN 978-0-9705889-0-6

Island Paradise Publishing All rights reserved.
P.O. Box 163
Haleiwa, Hi 96712
WWW.surfsupforkimo.com
Printed in China

First Edition - Sixth Printing

This story is dedicated to my son, Jack,
and all the children who live and surf on
the North Shore.

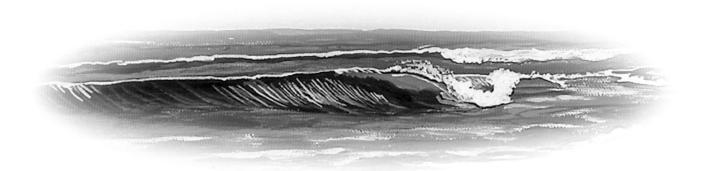

It was the day after Christmas on the North shore of O'ahu.

All the girls and boys were on their favorite playground,

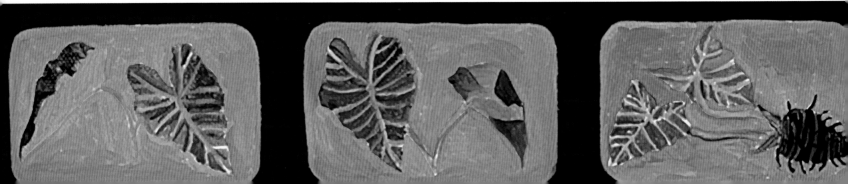

the ocean, trying out their new surfboards.

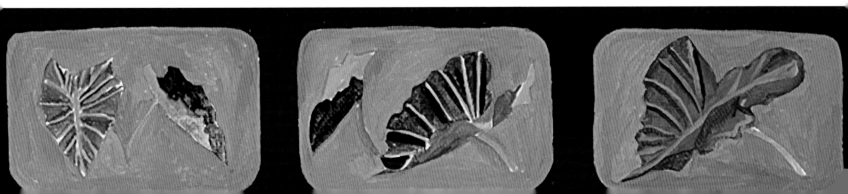

Five-and-half-year-old Kimo longed to be one of them.

Kimo wanted to be just like his older brothers.

They were two of the best surfers on the North Shore.

One day Kimo asked his oldest brother, "Kawika will you teach me to surf?"

"I was wondering when you would ask me that," said Kawika. "Sure I will."
"When can we start?" asked Kimo.

"Right now!" said Kawika. "The first step to becoming a surfer
is to become a strong swimmer."

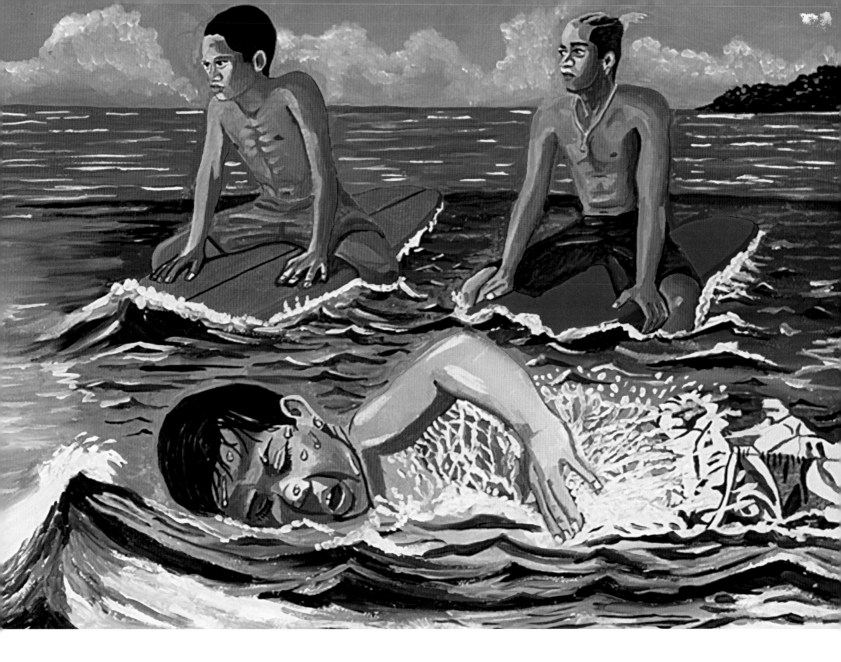

Kimo swam every day. When he was strong enough to
swim out to the surf line-up where his brothers sat on their
surfboards, he knew he was ready.

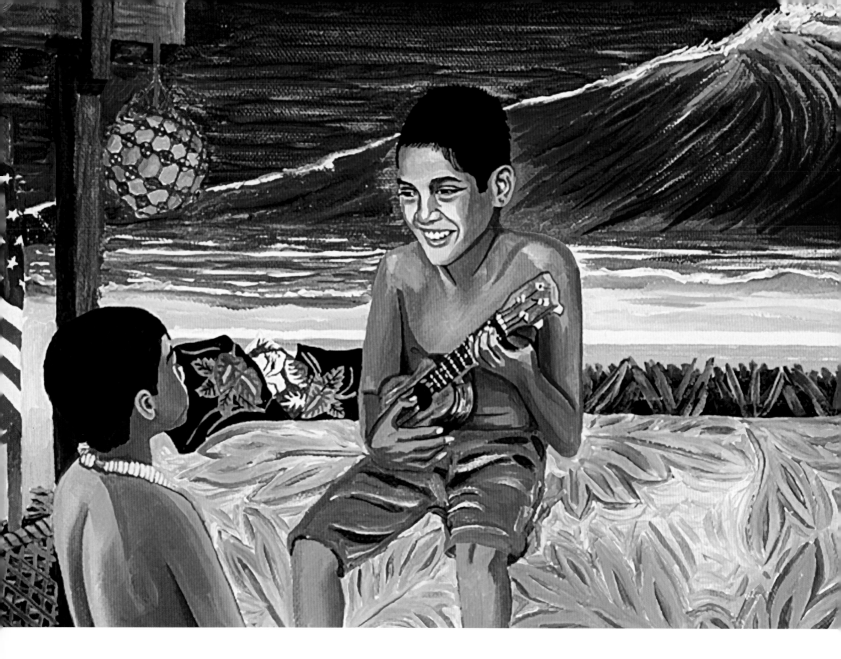

Kimo asked his brother Pono, "Will you teach me to surf
now that I am a strong swimmer?"

"I will Kimo," said Pono. "You've worked hard and soon you will be surfing. Now you are ready for the second step. Watch the waves so you will learn how they break."

Kimo watched the waves day in and day out. He watched
his brothers and where they sat on the ocean. They were
always in the perfect spot to catch the wave.

He watched his brothers glide across the turquoise waves,
flying from the top of the wave to the bottom.

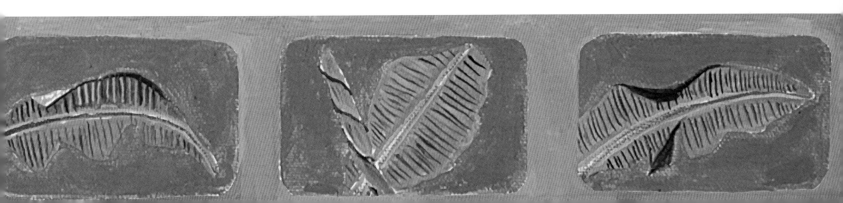

It looked like so much fun,

Kimo sometimes pretended he was the one riding the wave.

One afternoon, Kimo's mother said, " Kimo, you have been
studying those waves for hours. Why don't you come inside?
I have a story to tell you."
Kimo sighed. " But mom, how long will I have to watch
these waves before I can surf?"

"Not much longer," Kimo's mother said.
"When I was a little girl, I wanted to surf too."
"You did?."
"Yes, my sisters and brothers caught on faster than I did.
Then I remembered something."

"What did you remember?" asked Kimo.
"I remembered the stories my mother told me about not giving up.

When a wave came to me, one I knew was mine,
one with my name on it, I would say," `I can catch this wave,
I can catch this wave, and ride it all the way.'"

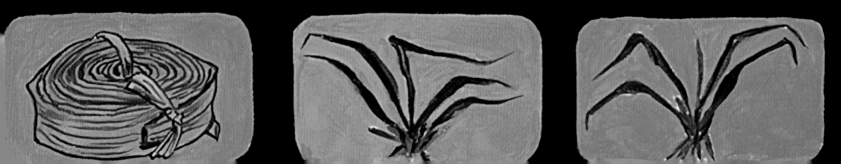

That night when Kimo went to bed, he dreamed about gliding across the turquoise waves, as he had dreamed many times before.

As he paddled for a wave in his dream, he said his mother's words. "I can catch this wave, I can catch this wave and ride it all the way."

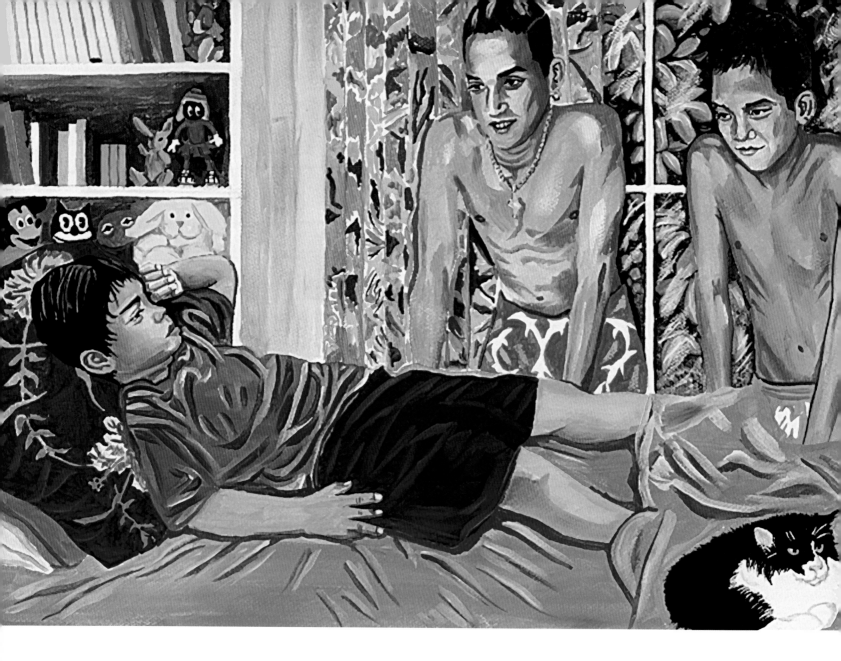

The next morning, Kimo awoke to find his two brothers staring him in the face. "Okay Kimo, are you ready to surf today?" they asked.

Kimo was so excited he jumped out of bed, threw on his swimming trunks, and ran for the beach.

When his brothers caught up with him, Pono handed him a surfboard.

"I learned on this board, then passed it on to Pono,"
Kawika said. "Now it's your's to learn on."
"Follow us out to the line-up!" yelled Pono as he dashed
for the water.

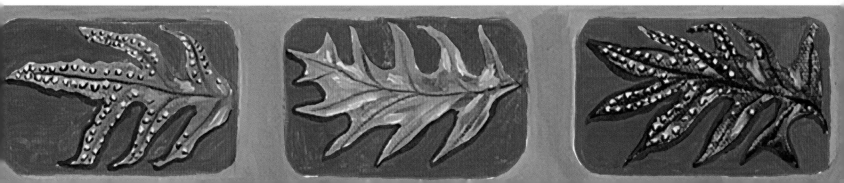

Kimo was happy to lie on the old, dinged board. He began
paddling just like his brothers. Paddling was harder than
it looked, but he kept going.

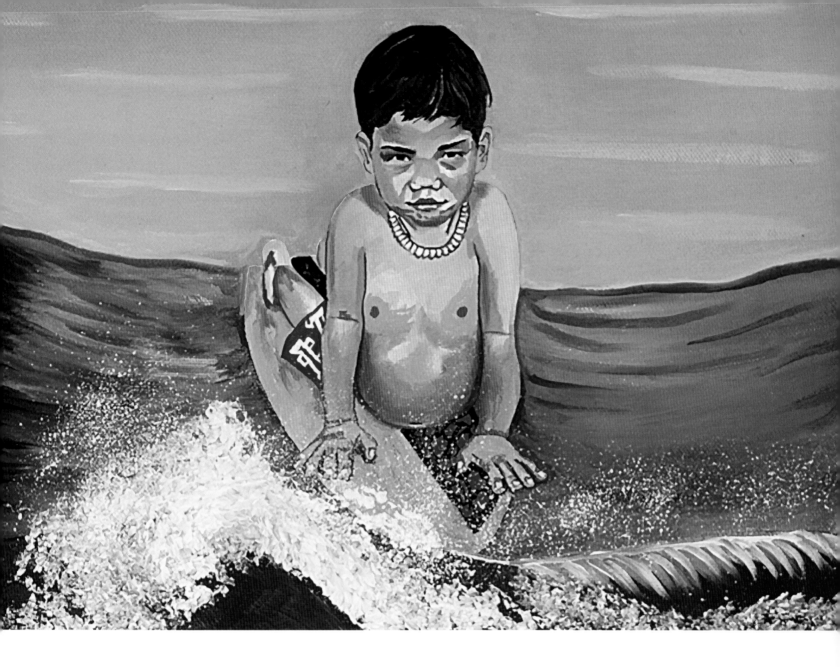

His arms ached by the time he reached the spot where the waves were breaking. He turned around, faced the beach, sat up on his board, and waited. When a wave came, he began paddling for it, but he couldn't catch it. Another wave came and another and another. Would he ever catch a wave?

Then Kimo heard another surfer say,
"Hey, kid, that one's got your name on it."
Then he remembered his mother's words. He began repeating.
"I can catch this wave, I can catch this wave and ride it all the way."

Before he knew it, he was up and riding the wave,
just like his brothers.

Across the turquoise wave he road, until he kicked out.
His brothers cheered and shouted. "All right Kimo!"
Kimo was stoked!

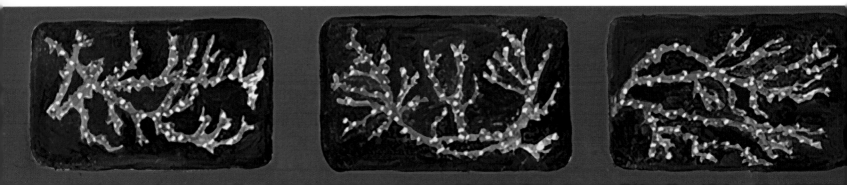

Kimo surfed every chance he got after that day, and just when he thought his life couldn't get any better...

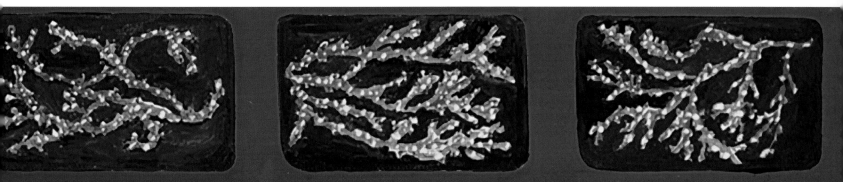

Christmas came around again bringing with it...

a brand new surf board.

ALOHA!

PRONUNCIATION GUIDE

Hawai'i State Flower

Here is a little something to help you with the Hawaiian words. The Hawaiian language is gentle and smooth to the ear. Whether you live here, on the mainland or abroad here are some guidelines to help you with this beautiful language.

Vowels
- A sounds like (ah) as in <u>a</u>bove.
- E sounds like (eh) as in w<u>e</u>t.
- I sounds like (ee) as in tr<u>ee</u>.
- O sounds like (oh) as in <u>o</u>bey.
- U sounds like (oo) as in d<u>u</u>de.

K and P   about the same as English but with less aspiration.

L,M,N,O   about the same as English.

W   Hawai'i (Hah wai ee) or (Ha vai ee) when w follows an a it sounds like w or v. Both are acceptable.

w   Hale'iwa (Hah lay eva) w after i sounds like v.

w   Kuwili (koo wee lee) w after u and o usually sounds like w.

The 'okina (glottal stop) is a consonant. It signifies a breath break "<u>Oh-oh</u>, I broke it."

Stress or accent in Hawaiian pronunciation is usually placed on the next to last syllable. An exception to the rule occurs when a Kahako (macron) (-) is shown above a vowel (mālolo), which is then treated with the greatest stress.

In 1978 it was declared that English and Hawaiian shall be the official languages of Hawai'i.

DID YOU FIND ANY OF THESE THINGS IN THE PICTURES?

Scrapper
This large cat is often seen on the beach in front of where he lives. He has been a member of the author's family for many years. How many times did you spot him?

Iwa bird
Haleʻiwa was named after this bird, hale (home) of the iwa, pronounced (eva) bird. Haleʻiwa town is located on the North Shore of Oʻahu.

Fishing float
Fishing floats still find their way to North shore beaches, brought by currents all the way from Japan. These glass balls are rare treasures from the sea.

Gecko
Hawaiʻi's favorite lizards are found everywhere. When you hear chuckling, it's probably a gecko laughing at you.

Flying fish (mālolo)
These fish are seen in outside waters. They rise out of the water and skim the tops of the waves. Their pectoral fins serve as wings, except they cannot move them as birds do.

Sand crab
These crabs dig large holes in the sand at night. If you look near the water's edge with a flashlight, you'll see one.

GLOSSARY

Page 1 ʻŌhelo berry
A native Hawaiian shrub. ʻŌhelo berries make delicious jams and jellies.

Page 2-3 Taro leaf (lau kalo)
The principal food of the Hawaiian people since their ancestors brought it to the islands centuries ago, taro is still actively farmed today. Poi, the pounded root of the taro leaf, is a favorite food of many children.

Page 4-5 Autograph tree
This shade tree is often planted around schoolyards. Kids sign their names on the leaves for others to see. They do this by scratching in the letters on the leaf with a stick.

Page 6-7 Hau leaf (lau hau)
This native hibiscus shrub has a one-day bloom. It opens yellow and turns pink before it drops. In the old days of Hawaiʻi, these branches were cut and stacked near the shoreline to tell people no fishing could be done there because the fish were spawning. Hauʻula town on the North Shore of Oʻahu was named after this shrub. It is also the home of the book's illustrator.

Page 8-9 Naupaku
This salt-tolerant shrub grows in sandy soil on or near the beach, commonly seen on the North Shore. Ancient Hawaiians used its leaves and bark for medicine.

Page 10-11 Coconut palm leaf (lau Nui)
This strong leaf is said to have the most uses of any leaf in the world. It is used for making houses, hats, baskets, furniture, mats, brooms, fans, ornaments, and musical instruments.

Page 12-13 Breadfruit (lau ulu)
The shape of this leaf is popular for designs on Hawaiian quilts and pillows. The wood from the breadfruit tree was favored by Hawaiians for it's lightness and strength in building decking for the great double-hulled canoes and for surfboards, small canoes and drums.

Page 14-15 Banana leaf (lau mai'a)
These leaves have lots of uses. A common use is to line the imu, an outside oven. The leaves act as a natural steamer for the food inside.
Our favorite use is to make banana bread with the fruit. Here is the author's recipe:

Banana Bread
Combine 3 cups flour • 2 T cinnamon • 1/2 t baking powder • 1t salt • 1t baking soda. Add 2 eggs • 2 sticks melted butter • 2 cups honey • 2 cups mashed banana • 3T vanilla.
Mix together well, pour in a buttered pan and bake at 325 degrees for one hour.

ACKNOWLEDGMENTS

I would like to thank my family, my friends,
and everyone who helped to make this storybook
a reality. My wonderful husband, Michael, who has
always encouraged and supported my ideas.
Vera Williams for bringing out the writer in me, along
with her continuous enthusiasm and support. The books
magnificent illustrator, Keoni Montes, for taking a chance
on me. His work brought Kimo to life in just the right way.
I'll always be so thankful for meeting and working with him.
Lynne, Elaine, Bob, Ellie and Nancy for the wonderful meetings
at Borders. Thank you for your gracious suggestions and editing.
To Kenny and Frank at K.W.A. Communications for their
patience and professionalism with this first timer.
Mahalo Nui Loa Kakou.

Aloha
Kerry Germain

Mahalo to my sweet wife Tina, who encouraged me
and stood by me through the worst of the "Starving Artist Days"
and my best buddy, Ed Rampell, for inspiring my artistic spirit!

Keoni Montes

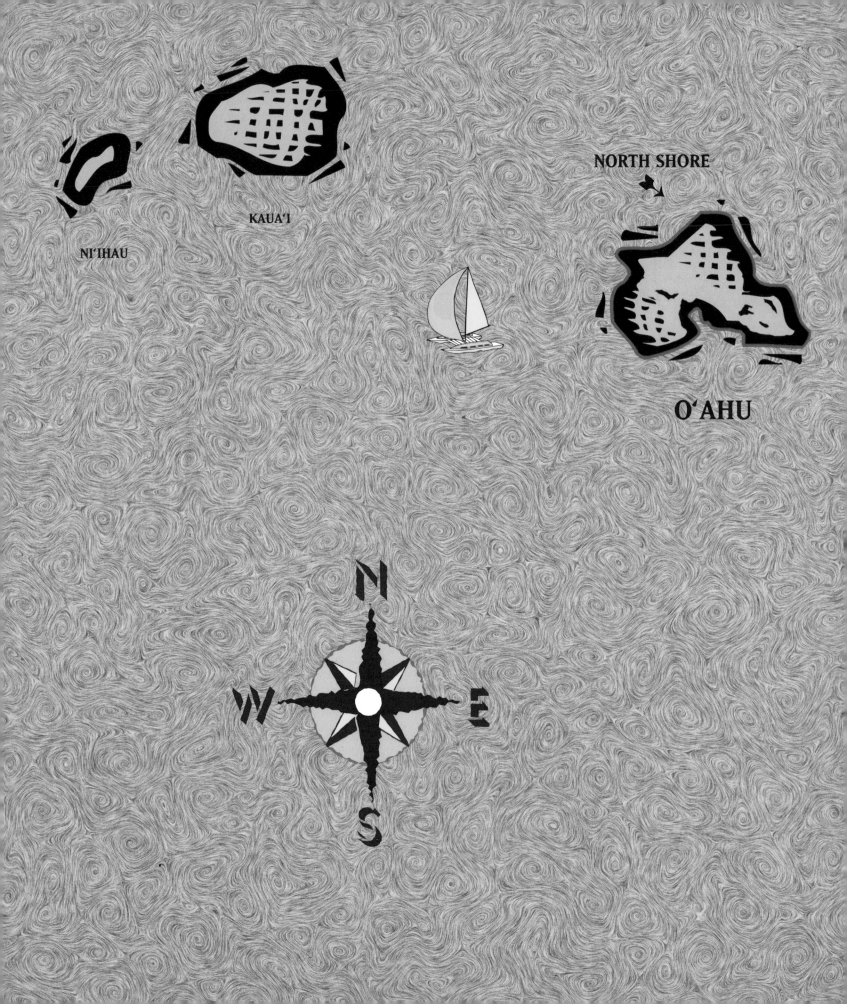

NI'IHAU

KAUA'I

NORTH SHORE

O'AHU

N

W   E

S